Pamela Binns is a character actress. She began her career at the David Garrick Theatre in Lichfield, the city where she was born and grew up. As well as stage plays, she has worked in radio (including four years in *Mrs Dale's Diary*) and TV and films. She acted with both Sean Connery and Sir Roger Moore before they became Bond. She played Queen Victoria in *Landseer* for BBC tv and was one of Richard Burton's many wives (Consuelo Vanderbilt) in the Son-et-Lumière for Blenheim Palace. Her latest role was in an episode of *Holby City* for BBC tv.

She has had many short stories and articles published and broadcast, and her previous cat book, *Flavio and the Cats of Rome*, was successfully published. She drives a seventeen-year-old Mini round London, where she lives with her tabby rescue cat, Perdita.

THE CHRISTMAS KITTENS

Pamela Binns

Book Guild Publishing

Sussex, England

First published in Great Britain in 2009 by
The Book Guild Ltd
Pavilion View
19 New Road
Brighton, BN1 1UF

Typesetting in Garamond by
SetSystems Ltd, Saffron Walden, Essex

Printed in Great Britain by
Athenaeum Press Ltd, Gateshead

A catalogue record for this book is
available from the British Library

ISBN 978 1 84624 346 2

*This book is dedicated to
the memory of Eileen,
who had the three kittens.*

Contents

Chapter 1

As We Were

My name is Polly. I have two brothers, Peter and Pipkin, and we're all stripey tabby kittens. Mrs Lovejoy says we're as alike as peas in a pod. It was because we all looked the same that some of the things happened. We're all very dark tabbies: our backs are black fur as soft as silk, and the rest of our fur is fawn with stripes. We all have white socklets on our front paws and longer white stockings on our back legs.

Of course our mother, Fozzy, knows which of us is which. (Fozzy's coat is black and white—our Dad must have been some tabby she met in Mrs Lovejoy's small walled back garden.) We were born in October, when the leaves were coming off the trees and fluttering against the windowpanes of Mrs Lovejoy's little terraced house. She lives on the outskirts of a small cathedral city. Round The Close, which surrounds the Cathedral, there are big grand houses, as I discovered much later. Where we lived wasn't like that. Mrs L.'s house was small and cosy, and we were all so happy.

We teased Fozzy by pretending we wanted to drink her

1

milk, although we'd been able to eat solid food for quite a while. We'd all got sharp little white teeth by then, which hurt poor Fozzy so that she knocked us away when we tried to suckle from her. That particular morning, undeterred by Fozzy's blow, Peter clambered up the blue velvet curtains and hung there, crying for help. I went to fetch Mrs Lovejoy, while Pipkin investigated to see if there was any food left in our breakfast dishes.

Mrs Lovejoy was wonderful—she always came when I called, so I managed to get her to leave the dishes and come to the rescue. As soon as she saw Peter—he was squeaking more loudly now, and hanging on by his front claws—she climbed briskly onto a chair and lifted him down. I purred my thanks round her ankles and Peter went off to join his brother in a search for food.

'You dratted kittens,' said Mrs Lovejoy, wiping her hands on her apron. (But she did give me a quick scratch behind the ears.) 'You've been bothering Fozzy again. You're too old for that. Quite time you kittens went. You can't stay here with me for ever, much as I'd like it. I can't possibly keep four cats, being on my own as I am. Besides, it wouldn't be fair on Fozzy.'

So she went and fetched her hat and coat and a warm pink scarf, as it was early December by then. She put her shopping bag over her arm and prepared to go out.

'Now you be good,' she said to us. She didn't need to include Fozzy in that instruction—our mother was the most beautifully behaved cat in Milchester. 'I'm going to put a

notice in the corner shop—"Good Homes Wanted"—for you lot. We'll just have to see what answers we get.' And with that she went out of the blue front door, closing it carefully behind her.

At that time we didn't really know what a good home was, and I didn't realise how lucky we were to be loved and fed and petted and cared for. I was soon going to learn the hard way. But that morning, while Mrs L. was away on her mysterious errand, and Fozzy had retired upstairs for a good wash and a snooze, Peter had discovered Mrs L.'s knitting. For the next half-hour we all enjoyed the most wonderful romp unravelling it. And though we didn't know it, all our play was teaching us to pounce and capture for a time when our lives might depend on such skills.

When she returned, Mrs L. was not pleased at the mess we'd made.

'Quite time you lot went,' she repeated firmly, gathering up the shredded remnants of wool that was all that remained of the jumper she'd been making. She put the scraps back into her knitting bag and snapped it shut.

Then she served us our supper before she had hers. I forgot to mention that all three of us have heart-shaped white bib markings. Fozzy taught us to wash them until they sparkled, especially after we'd had a good meal. So that was what we did.

Chapter 2

The Mysterious Stranger

It was the next evening, and now it was winter the afternoon darkness had closed in early. As she drew the blue velvet curtains in the living room, I noticed Mrs Lovejoy watching a few snow flakes drifting down. She shivered, and twitched the curtains still more firmly into place. We were all warm and cosy. The real fire in the grate had been burning merrily all day.

'Tea, everyone?' said Mrs. L. 'Who shall I serve first?' Which was her little joke, because we knew our delicious meal came while she waited for the kettle to boil for her brew. 'Polly put the kettle on?' she asked me, but I preferred to stay by the fire. Peter had discovered his own tail, and was spinning round and round trying to catch it. Pipkin was patting one of the little balls Mrs L. had given us to play with.

Fozzy was dozing beside me on the hearth rug. Her eyes were half shut, as she pretended she wasn't watching us. But if we'd done anything too outrageous she'd have batted us with a strong paw to keep us in order.

Suddenly there was a knock at the front door. I think at that moment we all jumped. Mrs L. didn't have many visitors, and no one ever called at that time of the evening. Nevertheless, she went to open the door, and I knew, with a strange quivering feeling that went from my whiskers to the tip of my tail, that something terrible was going to happen. For the first time in my life I found myself growling.

Our mistress flung open the door. A tall man stood there—he was wearing a black fedora hat bespeckled with flecks of snow. There were snowflakes, too, on the wide shoulders of his black cloak. Behind him the snow was falling even more heavily, so that he appeared like a huge dark shadow against the whiteness. His face was long and ended in a short pointed black beard. Although I couldn't see them, I felt sure his eyes were that colour, too. But the most sinister thing of all was the covered black box he was carrying.

The stranger leant over Mrs Lovejoy (who wasn't very tall) and said in a deep voice, 'I've come for the kittens.'

At the menacing sound of his voice, Fozzy fled from the room to seek refuge under the bed upstairs, leaving us to our fate. Moving as one, the three of us scuttled for the only safety we knew—underneath the sofa. We snuggled against each other's fur for comfort and reassurance. We hardly dared to breathe, but our ears were cocked to hear everything that was said.

But our dear owner was still standing in the doorway, dumbfounded.

'May I come in?' asked the mysterious stranger, removing

8

his hat with a sweeping bow. 'You have the kittens, I presume? By a happy coincidence I happened to be in this part of the world, and I saw your advertisement. I was visiting my mother. And it so happens I need some kittens.'

'Yes, but . . .' Poor Mrs Lovejoy had no idea how to handle this unexpected situation.

Now the stranger was standing straddled in front of the fire as if he owned the room. His cloak was thrown back, revealing the scarlet lining.

'Might I perhaps see the animals in question?'

Squeezed as we were under the sofa, I could hear Peter's heart beating wildly on my left, and on my right Pipkin's breath was coming in little short frightened pants.

'I really don't think they're old enough to leave home,' was the only excuse Mrs L. could think of. She certainly didn't want this sinister man to have any of her lovely kittens.

'Ten weeks, your advertisement stated. I believe that's the correct age for them to be taken away from their mother. They must be pestering her now?'

'Well—yes—but . . .' Mrs Lovejoy's reply was hesitant, but she really couldn't think of any other excuses. After all, she *had* advertised for homes. So, down on her knees she went and pulled us out from our dark hiding place.

The stranger snatched Peter from her hands and held him up by his tail. Peter squawked loudly at the indignity, but he was also very frightened.

'He's male. I'll take him.' He snapped open the cage, and a howling and protesting Peter began his imprisonment. The

same crude business was repeated with Pipkin, and once his sex had been affirmed he joined his brother in the terrifying box.

I was shaking with fear when it was my turn for the terrible inspection.

'A female—no use to me. Girls get nervy and temperamental. You can keep her. The other two'll do fine—boys are much steadier. And them looking so alike, that's a real bonus. Here—' He produced his wallet and a large note was stuffed in Mrs L.'s unwilling hand.

'No, no, thank you, but I don't want . . . I wouldn't dream of taking money for them. In fact, I really don't want . . .'

In shock and horror, I'd once more taken refuge under the sofa, but I could still see and hear what was going on.

The lid of the dark box containing my two brothers was firmly closed and the fedora with the wide brim was back on the sinister man's head. He was putting on his leather gloves again as Mrs Lovejoy, still protesting, opened the front door for him. Then the wallet was produced once more.

'I nearly forgot,' said the man. 'I must give you my card.' He pressed it into her hand and then disappeared into the night and the swirling snow.

Mrs Lovejoy was sobbing as she closed the door. I watched her move to the fireplace. Suddenly she was aware of the money in her hand, and without a moment's hesitation, she dropped the note into the flames. I saw, as she did not, the pasteboard visiting card the man had given her fall from her hand into the fire as well.

I felt it was safe to come out and try and comfort my lovely owner. She was still crying, and I rubbed round her ankles, purring as best I could. (It was a fairly new accomplishment of mine.) Mrs Lovejoy picked me up and held me close to her face. She stroked my soft stripey fur.

'Oh, little Polly, what've I done to Peter and Pipkin? I shouldn't have let him take them like that. What's he going to do with them? What did he want them for? He was so scary, I was downright frightened of him. And to think I'd take money for my little darlings . . . Who was he, anyway? Where's that card he gave me? I had it in my hand. Oh, no, I can't have burnt it? Now I'll never know where they've gone. I'll never see them again. Oh my dear Peter and Pipkin . . .'

How could I tell her that I had indeed seen our only chance of finding out where my brothers had gone devoured by the flames?

That night I was very lonely. Fozzy went upstairs with Mrs Lovejoy, and I slept on my own for the first time in my life.

13

Chapter 3

Escape, and I Meet a Posh Cat

I didn't sleep a wink that night. I missed the furry comfort of my brothers—we'd always slept cuddled close to each other. Now they were gone, and we didn't know where. The slip of pasteboard that would have told us their whereabouts had been accidentally burnt.

As the long hours of the night ticked by, I went over all the horrors of the previous evening: the terrible dark stranger who had seemed sinister to me from the moment he stood in the doorway—even as I thought of him, a shiver of fear engulfed me; the way his huge hands had roughly pushed my brothers into the dark box; and his strange departure, without explanation, into the night.

Where, oh where had he taken my brothers, and why? I tried licking my little white paws for comfort, and wondered if Peter and Pipkin were doing the same thing. Were they warm, like me? The fire had died down, but the glowing coals still gave off enough heat for me to be comfortable. Were they hungry—empty—starving? My white belly was

15

round and stretched; despite my upset I'd managed to eat most of my supper. (But how lonely it'd been: I'd had the heaped plate all to myself, without Peter and Pipkin leaving theirs and trying to take from mine, as they always did.)

But the more I thought about it, the more puzzled I became. What had happened was *no good*. And the sinister gentleman was certainly not offering them *good homes*. Fozzy had warned us about strangers who scooped kittens up in the streets. I started shivering and I couldn't stop. According to our mother, there were two reasons kittens were kidnapped: for their fur or for biological experiments. My whiskers twitched in agitation as I faced the awful truth.

What could I do? The man's name and address had been lost in the flames. I only knew I had to save my brothers from their dreadful fate. I was their sister, and we'd always been a threesome. I must discover where they were and rescue them. Quite how I was going to do this I hadn't a clue. But with my mind made up, I was able to have a short catnap until Mrs Lovejoy came to open the curtains and rake out the ashes.

She picked me up and hugged me as she always did. (Before, she'd hugged my brothers as well.)

For a moment I thought she'd forgotten the awful happenings of the previous night. But, holding me against her cheeks, she whispered, 'Oh, Polly, Polly, where are they? I shouldn't have let them go like that. As for burning the money, how could I have been so foolish? I could've given it to charity. That's what I should have done . . .'

Then Fozzy came down, loudly demanding her breakfast.

She wasn't too concerned about Peter and Pipkin's departure. She'd had kittens before and off they went to new homes when they reached the right age. She said, as we both wolfed down our coley, that she couldn't understand why Mrs L. and I were both so worried. I tried to explain about the cold shivers the man had given me. I didn't dare to voice my worst fears, so I concentrated on eating. I was going to go on a long and hazardous search and I needed to start building up my strength.

I had to plan running away very carefully. Obviously Mrs Lovejoy would be distraught at my disappearance. Even Fozzy, for all her apparent lack of concern about Peter and Pipkin's removal, was hardly likely to help her daughter to go off and look for them.

It was a long time until my chance to escape came. The blue front door remained firmly closed, like all the windows, now it was winter. But suddenly I saw the opportunity I needed, and I seized it with all paws. The travelling fishmonger, who visited once a month, called with his van. It was about noon, and he was knocking on the door and Mrs L. opened it.

'Morning, Mrs L. Usual, is it? Only I've got some lovely fresh prawns I thought I might tempt you with. Might you be interested?'

'Oh, Mr Pike, I forgot it was your day. I'll just go and get my purse. Then it'll be the usual—though just a little bit less for the cats. Excuse me a moment.'

'How is them lovely little pussies then?' enquired the fishmonger.

And as Mrs L. went into the kitchen to fetch her purse from the kitchen dresser, this little pussy slipped out and past Mr Pike, who was doing up the delicious-smelling parcel and didn't see me.

I had escaped! I ran and ran up the road, and, still galloping, turned into the next one, and then right again. The pavement was hard under my sensitive paws, and my heart seemed to be pounding against my ribs. I had to pause to get my breath.

A young woman pushing a pram saw me and stooped down to talk.

'Issums a little pussy den? Issums lost?'

I cowered back against a wall. Luckily at that moment the baby started to cry and her attention was diverted. I darted away.

I soon realised what a liability human beings were going to be. I suppose I was quite a small, rather attractive tabby kitten, but everyone I met on the streets either wanted to adopt me or take me to the police station (whatever that was). Or generally interfere with my plans. Everyone thought I was a stray, but all I wanted to do was find my brothers and save them.

So I decided to go where human beings couldn't. I took to the cats' pathways. I had to scramble and clamber to get to the top of the wall (I wasn't very big then), but once I was up on the cats' roadways, the city opened up before me. Wall led to wall, and then sometimes connected to a low balcony. I hurried along—I was feeling safer now, away from the grasping human hands that tried to capture me. Sometimes it was white modern breeze blocks under my paws, sometimes beautiful old red bricks. I had no idea where I was going, but all the time I knew I was being led.

Eventually I arrived in a picturesque garden in the middle of a square surrounded by enormous houses. I jumped off the wall, landing gently as Fozzy had taught us, and sauntered between the flower beds. These were winter-bare now, but here and there the black soil was topped with frost that was melting in the faint afternoon sunlight.

I skipped down some stone steps that were sunk into the grass, and there, sitting on the paved slabs surrounding an ancient sundial, was a huge grey Persian cat. His long coat was perfectly groomed, and he was surveying the garden with the utmost disdain. I gave a little jump of surprise, and lowered my tail. The Persian cat spoke.

'Come here, you common little kitten, and tell me what you are doing in this *private* garden. Did you know you're trespassing? This is *my* garden.'

I shook my head dumbly. I'd never met any cats except my own dear family. This one, whose voice was a cross between a purr and a growl, seemed very strange to me. And rather frightening.

I crept towards him, keeping my body very close to the damp stones.

'I'm very sorry your . . .' (I wondered if I should call him 'Highness'. He seemed kingly enough.) I finally settled for 'Lordship' and this seemed to please the well-bred cat.

He ordered me to come and sit beside him. Taking a few more tentative steps, I did so. The gentleman relaxed a little, and even gave my head a few gentle licks.

'Well, what are you doing here?' he repeated more kindly.

I suddenly felt very hungry and lonely and far from home. Before I knew it the whole story came tumbling out—how I didn't know what had happened to my brothers and I was afraid they'd met some dreadful fate. By the end of my tale I was shiving with agitation.

The Persian cat didn't seem to know how to answer. He filled in the time, as we cats do, by licking his already lustrous coat. When he did speak, his words came very slowly.

'Urchin kitten, I just might be able to help you. My master—by the way, we live in that white house there—is the cleverest man in Milchester. Of course that is why he chose me to live with him. He works very hard. But when he comes home at night, after he's dined, he sits in his study in front of this machine. When he presses the keys, the answers to all his questions come up on the screen in front of him. Now suppose I asked his machine where your brothers are—I might be able to get some information about them.'

'Could you, would you?' I couldn't conceal my eagerness.

The Persian cat went on talking in his growly voice.

'Before I try to do this, you'd have to do something for me. A little favour, you might call it.'

'But what would you want me to do for you?' I asked anxiously.

'It would be such a little thing for a common kitten like

you to accomplish. Something, I'm sure, you do almost every day of your life. Talking of my master's dinner reminded me of my failing appetite. Believe me, there is no shortage of salmon and trout and grouse and cream in my house, but sometimes I find myself craving for something rather different. What did you eat in your pokey little home, kitten?'

'Mrs Lovejoy gave us lovely food. Cat food. She bought it in tins and packets from the corner shop. And coley from Mr Pike the fishmonger. We never went short of anything.'

The big cat moved his head so that his huge orange eyes came very close to my face.

'But did you never taste—mice?' he whispered.

I recoiled at this strange request. Fozzy had caught a mouse, once, in Mrs Lovejoy's little walled garden. Our mother had played with it for more than an hour—tossing it in the air and calling us to come and join her game. But Mrs. L. had kept us firmly indoors, and had finally taken her plaything away from a disgusted Fozzy. The corpse disappeared, I don't know where.

Now this stranger was demanding a mouse in return for helping to discover the whereabouts of my brothers. I wanted help so badly. I didn't know what to say. I nibbled at my paws and wondered how I might find a mouse, let alone kill one.

'It's my teatime. I'll leave you to think about our bargain.'

The aristocratic cat arched his fluffy back and extended each silken paw as he stretched himself.

'See you back here at the sundial sometime. I'm here most

23

days, weather permitting, of course. Bring me a morsel of mouse and I'll see if I can locate your brothers. I wonder what they're going to tempt me with for tea today . . .'

And he sauntered away, his great bushy tail held proudly aloft.

I crouched down on the hard paving stones. I felt very small and very, very hungry. And I hadn't the faintest idea how I could catch a mouse in order to get this strange cat to help me in my search for Peter and Pipkin.

Chapter 4

Mr Reynard-Fox and the Party

But it was no use sitting in the garden feeling hungry and sorry for myself. I set off once again, not knowing where I was going. I hadn't the faintest idea how I might find and catch a mouse. All the rest of the day I roamed the cats' roads of the city. I ran across walls and fences and, occasionally, greatly daring, crept along a balcony.

While crossing one of these, I was almost overcome by the smell drifting from the house. The odour of whatever was cooking was so delicious I was tempted to press my face against the window and plead to be let in. But I checked this impulse. 'Polly,' I scolded myself, 'somehow you've got to keep going.'

The short winter afternoon had drawn in and it was nearly dark when I returned to street level. I felt safer in the dusk. I was drawn to some dustbins outside a house. There, and oh, the joy of it, were the half-eaten remains of a takeaway, carelessly thrown about. At Mrs Lovejoy's I would have turned my nose up at such discarded fare. Now I wolfed the lot, not caring what it was nor where it came from. There was a lime tree by the bins, and I settled down among its roots to give myself a good wash and brush up after my stolen meal. I felt heavy and replete, but I started licking one white-socked paw.

Suddenly I heard a gruff voice behind me.

'Whatcher up to, little kit-cat? Pinched me dinner, 'ave yer?'

The speaker was a fox, though I didn't know it until he introduced himself. Which he did, rather more politely than the Persian cat in the garden had done. Through the failing light I was able to make out his somewhat matted red-brown coat and his full brush tail. He stared at me with fierce yellow eyes.

'My name's Reynard-Fox, at your service. And what's a young kit like yerself doin' out at this time o' night? Yer should be safely tucked up at 'ome, shouldn't yer? Where is yer home then?'

A note of kindness had crept into his hoarse voice, and suddenly everything became too much for me. I shivered and whimpered, and my breath came in great heaving sobs. Why was I on this silly quest? Peter and Pipkin were probably already dead. I longed to be safely at home with Fozzy beside me and Mrs Lovejoy to look after me.

'There, there, little 'un, don't take on. There's no problem that can't be solved. Tell yer Uncle Reynard all about it.'

And the fox settled down beside me. I was glad of the warmth, but to tell the truth there was a strong odour from

26

his body that was far from pleasant. But, stammering at first, I told him all that had happened.

'A mouse, eh? For want o' a mouse the trail goes cold. Never fear, yer new friend Reynard can 'elp. 'Ee knows where mice can be 'ad for the pickin'. Just leave it to me. *Au revoir, ma petite amie* . . .'

And with those strange but comforting words, the fox slunk off into the darkness.

At that point I must have fallen asleep. I was woken up by a young woman's high voice.

'Look Miles, a kitten. Do come and look, she's adorable.'

A soft hand caressed my head. It was good to be fondled again. A young man was now peering at me as well, but it was the girl who kept talking.

'Isn't she the sweetest thing you ever saw?'

By now she was holding me against her cheek—her black hair tickled. I let all my paws go limp—what a mistake!

'She is rather cute, I'll admit that.'

'But she's lost, Miles, she's definitely lost. What's she doing sleeping by our bins? I'm going to adopt her.'

'You can't do that, Tara. She probably belongs to someone else. I expect she's got a very good home the other side of town, and she's just wandered off and got lost.'

The young woman tossed her straight dark hair. It was cut fairly short, with a fringe that came down to her arched eyebrows.

'I don't believe it. She's a homeless stray and I'm keeping her. You know I've always wanted a cat.'

28

'Tara, you can't do this . . .'

By now the girl was clutching me defensively. Too late, I realised what was happening. I dug my claws into her vivid red coat, but to no avail. The young man, who was wearing a smart dark blue suit, realised it was useless to argue. He'd gone up the six steps and was opening the front door of the Victorian house. The girl followed, holding me in a vice-like grip, for I was struggling for my freedom. Up and up the green-carpeted stairs we went. My head swam. The couple lived in the flat at the very top of the house. With a cold shudder I heard their front door close behind me. I was a prisoner.

Being held captive in a flat was the last thing I wanted. How stupid I'd been to let myself get caught like that. The girl plonked me down in their bare open-plan living space. The floor was polished wood, and as I tried to run for safety my paws skidded away from me.

'Oh, look—she's skating!' giggled Tara, subsiding into a very strange-looking chair made of glass and metal.

I was so frightened—there was nowhere to hide, and it was so different from Mrs Lovejoy's home. I cringed in a corner, still shaking with fright.

'Well, now you've brought her up here you'd better give her something to eat,' suggested the fair-haired young man. 'Before we start getting ready for the party,' he added ominously.

Tara made her way to the kitchen area, which was at the front of the flat.

29

'What d'you think she'd fancy? Raspberries, peanut butter, olives?'

'Oh, for heaven's sake, Tara.' Miles strode over to the fridge and peered in. 'Here, give the poor little thing some smoked salmon.'

'But that's for the canapés tonight.'

'If you have a pet, you've got to feed it. And properly. And look after it. Tara, I don't think you've thought this thing through. We're both out at work all day, and this isn't a suitable flat for a kitten.' He went on, 'So, we leave the trapdoor open for her and she's going to go running up and down the iron staircase? And there's also the little matter that almost certainly she belongs to someone else.'

'Nonsense. She's a stray in need of a good home. I can sense it.'

'We'll have to make some enquiries. Find out who the local vet is, and take her to see if she's microchipped. Or someone may have reported losing her.'

'But not till after Christmas.'

'I suppose not, it's getting near. Now for goodness' sake, feed the poor little thing and let's start preparing for the party.'

So I got my smoked salmon (on a rather peculiar square plate) and although I wasn't terribly hungry I ate most of it. I was still crouching by the wall, as there wasn't anywhere to hide. Miles busied himself putting out glasses; my eyes widened at the number of bottles he produced. Mrs L. sometimes had a sherry on Sundays, I'd sniffed the glass when

30

she left it on the floor, but I'd never seen anything like this layout. Tara was busy making the eats. But several times she came over and picked me up, squeezing me uncomfortably.

'Oozums a good pussy den? Oozums going to enjoy the party?'

No, I certainly was not going to enjoy the party. I had to escape, but how? There was only one door to the flat and that was firmly shut. Even if I could get out and down all those stairs, the front door of the building would certainly be closed. My heart sank. Rescuing my brothers seemed a distant dream. Now I needed rescuing myself.

The doorbell went, and the first guests arrived. At last I managed to find a hiding place. I squeezed myself in behind a big box from which loud music was blaring. More and more people arrived, and the room gradually filled up. The noise and chatter grew steadily louder until I could barely hear myself think. I was desperate. Through all the shrieking I suddenly heard a shrill female voice asking to go up to the roof garden. Someone—was it Miles?—went up the metal staircase and then there was the sound of the trapdoor being opened.

I seized my chance and dashed from my hiding place across the room. But it was no good. A plump young woman caught me and held me up, although I fought as hard as I could, lashing out with my claws in every direction.

'What a darling kitten, Tara! You never said you'd got it.'

The girl was swaying slightly—I began to feel seasick. Then she offered me an olive from the plate beside her and, being foolish, I tried to swallow it. It stuck in my throat and the result was quick. As I hadn't been groomed for some time there was also a fur ball waiting to come out. I started to rasp horribly, the prelude to being sick. The girl hastily put me down and the vomit and fur ball came out onto the polished floorboards. A few specks went on the girl's modish black dress.

'Ugh! Tara—just look what your horrid little pet's done!'

'Oh, Felicity, I'm so sorry—let me wipe your dress. Miles, clear up that disgusting mess!'

No one was the least concerned about me. So, fuelled by panic and fear, I made a bolt through all the guests for the metal staircase. It was terribly difficult for me, a small kitten, to climb the iron rungs. But as I was desperate I managed somehow.

Only one guest noticed my departure in the general hullabaloo.

'There she blows,' he cried drunkenly. 'I mean, goes . . .'

But I made it to the top of the ladder. I was out on the asphalt flooring of the roof garden, under the stars. It was bitterly cold. I shivered as I inspected the various boxes and containers that in the summer would hold plants. I went to the very edge of the roof in each direction. There was no way down.

If cats could cry, I would have wept then. I seemed to have got into a hopeless situation from which there was no escape. Throughout the long cold night I patrolled the roof, peering over the sheer drop of five storeys from either end. And

sideways, where the house joined its neighbours, was a high, unclimbable wall surrounded by chimney pots. I crouched in the shadow of a large box of evergreen shrubs and for a short time I dozed off. But there was no protection from the bitter wind that swept over the rooftops. A crescent moon rode through the skies. When I caught glimpses of her, between the clouds, I prayed to her as my Egyptian ancestors had done. (I didn't consciously know this—it was an inborn knowledge inherited by all cats.) I asked for release from my desolate state, and for help and guidance to escape so that I could continue my quest for my brothers, whose fate was surely worse than mine.

At last I could bear the cold no longer. Perhaps the Moon Goddess heard the prayer of a little tabby kitten stranded on a rooftop. Stealthily, crouching low, I inched my way to the trapdoor. It was still open, but there was a strange silence from the flat below. And a strange smell that I couldn't identify. My nostrils twitched—it was a distinctly unpleasant odour. Gingerly I put one white-tipped paw on the top rung of the iron ladder, followed by my other front paw. Going down was harder than climbing up, but I reached the second rung from the bottom and jumped to the floor.

The floor was strewn with the bodies of the party guests. They lay about, some singly, others in pairs. And everywhere there was this very strong smell. I sprang over a few of the bodies. As I leapt over one young man he opened an eye and took a swipe at me. I took the opportunity to have a quick pee.

34

'Help! It's raining in here!' he cried, half sitting up. 'Help! A tiger's come to get me!'

He fell back onto the floor with a crash.

Jumping like a racehorse over hurdles, I made for the door. I couldn't believe my luck—it was standing open! Some of the leaving partygoers must have left it ajar. I dashed through and down the first flight of green-carpeted stairs.

On the next landing I paused. I needed to stop and think about my situation. While I thought, I began to wash myself carefully, starting by licking my front paw and bringing it over my ears, just as Fozzy had taught us. I'd got as far as fully extending my right hind leg so that I could wash my nether regions, when a dreadful thought struck me: what if the party guests hadn't left the street door open? What if one of the other residents had closed it? Was I still trapped?

I galloped down the remaining flights of stairs. My worst fears were realised; the front door was shut. There was no way that I, a small kitten could possibly open it.

The dawn was coming and it was growing light. Soon it would be morning, and just on the other side of the door the fox would return with my mouse. The mouse which was going to bribe the arrogant cat to consult his master's machine. Which just might tell me where I could find Peter and Pipkin.

Chapter 5

I Make a Delivery and a Discovery

For no reason that I could explain, I returned to the second-floor landing. There was an aura of safety about it. This didn't disappear when the door of the flat on that landing slowly opened. An old woman stood there. Her grey hair was scraped back into an untidy bun, and her clothes were long and dark. She was leaning on a stick.

'Oh, kitten, what are you doing here? Was the party too much for you? It was for me. But I expect you want to be away and on with your business, is that it?'

There was something of Mrs Lovejoy's kindness about the old lady. But through my adventures I had already learnt to be wary of strangers. I must not get trapped again. I edged away, retreating down a couple of stairs.

'Oh yes, you want to get out, don't you? You certainly don't belong in this house. My goodness, you're so pretty. Someone must be missing you. Come and have a bite to eat and then I'll see you on your way.'

The old lady's voice was so encouraging that I took a few

tentative steps into her flat. The living room was warm and cosy—it reminded me of Mrs Lovejoy's house. But there were stars all over the floor, and that puzzled me. The stars I knew were in the heavens to guide little cats, or others that were lost.

The old lady, the rubber ferule on the end of her stick beating lightly on the floor, produced a plate of finely chopped chicken and a saucer of water. I drank thirstily, and devoured the meal. And all the while the old woman talked to me in her cracked, crooning voice.

'D'you like my stars, little kitten? Other people have them up above, but for me they are down here on earth. They tell me things that are not ours to question. You still have far to travel in your quest, little kitten. You will go into a great stone building filled with singing and music. But in the end you will see your brothers again.'

I purred my thanks by rubbing against her black-stockinged legs.

'You want to be off now, little kitten, don't you? Joy in your journeying. We shan't meet again but I will think of you. Come with me now.'

She opened the door, and together we made our way down the stairs, she limping, me skipping, from step to step. She opened the front door, and I knew she was watching me as I ran to the linden tree where Reynard was waiting.

'Where've you bin, kitty-kat?' asked the fox, flicking his bushy tail over his neat black back legs. His pong was stronger than ever, so I didn't lie down too close to him. I

told him my story as hurriedly as I could. Mr Reynard gave something resembling a growl, and showed his sharp teeth.

'Main thing is, yer got away from their clutches. An' by-the-by, I got somefink fer yer—though by rights I was thinkin', I should've been teachin' yer to do it yerself. That's all the rage now, innit—do-it-yerself?' Then he cautiously lifted a forepaw to reveal the squashed corpse of what must have once been a mouse. '*Voilà*, as they say in that French caff where there's the best pickin's in the 'igh Street. An' I should know. I'm the king o' the bin bags round 'ere.'

'I don't know how to thank you,' I purred, reaching out a tentative paw.

The fox snapped his jaws. For an awful moment I thought what a good meal *I'd* make for him. I decided to get away as soon as possible. I clutched the corpse in my mouth; it tasted rancid and I did wonder where Reynard had caught it. I turned to go.

'*Adieu, ma chère amie.*' Although he'd been so kind to me, I didn't altogether trust the fox's fierce glinting eyes. I trotted away as quickly as I could.

It was difficult to find my way back to the garden. There were so many walls, so many cats' walkways. But at last I reached it, and there, basking in the pale winter sunshine by the sundial, lay the posh Persian cat.

'Thought you were never coming, young lady,' he said, extending an elegant paw. 'You young things—out on the tiles, were you?'

I was about to answer, 'In a manner of speaking, yes,' when

he interrupted me with a hiss. 'Have you brought me my mouse?'

I dropped the sodden corpse under his nose. For a moment or two he played with it idly, as if he'd caught it himself. He tossed it in the air a few times, but soon grew tired of his game.

'Now I shall try to eat this delicacy,' he announced, and sank his teeth (I noticed one or two were missing) into the brown fur. For a few minutes he chewed determinedly, but then he spat out the remains.

'That was disgusting,' he declared. 'But at least I can say I've tasted mouse.' He paused, deep in thought, but at last he continued. 'Well, my little friend. You kept your side of the bargain, and now I suppose I must keep mine. I'll have to try to help you in your ridiculous quest to find your brothers. Follow me, if you please, young lady.'

He led the way across the garden to one of the magnificent houses that bordered the square. I was relieved to see there was a cat flap on the front door. An easy escape route, I hoped. I also noted it was an extra-large one to accommodate His Lordship, who now butted it with his head and entered the house. We crossed the hallway of black-and-white tiles, a giant chessboard for giant players. In the silence a grandfather clock ticked sonorously.

We went down a long corridor, and the Persian cat turned into a room at the back of the house—the door was conveniently ajar for us. But what a room—the soft carpet was like springing grass under my pads. I sniffed at the bottom of the velvet curtains, many times thicker than those in Mrs Lovejoy's front room. I was assailed by all the different scents that came to me. There were exotic flowers in vases, even though it was mid-winter. I explored the plush upholstered sofa and matching armchairs. I wandered about the room, sniffing and smelling everything that was so grand and strange.

Meanwhile the Persian cat had leapt, or rather heaved himself, onto a curious high metal chair. It was placed in front of the machine he'd told me about. This was like a slim open suitcase, with what I recognised as typewriter keys in front of it. (Dear Mrs L. used to type some of her letters on one.) The screen was all lit up—obviously the big cat's master left it switched on. The Persian cat stared at the screen for a few moments, and then, with great deliberation, he raised a furry forepaw and struck two or three of the typewriter keys. The picture changed, and the Persian cat hit several more keys. The screen turned into a white sheet. The arrogant one muttered to himself. A few black squiggles appeared on the blank screen in front of him.

'What is it saying?' I asked hopefully. Of course I can't read, but I thought perhaps it was an art this enormously clever cat had mastered. (From his still cleverer master? I wondered.) A few more characters appeared on the screen, and the big cat swore to himself between his broken teeth. I began to suspect that he couldn't read either, and, losing interest, I wandered about the room.

There was another box in an alcove that I hadn't noticed before. It was rather similar to the one Mrs Lovejoy had in her living room. Mrs L. sometimes watched the moving pictures on it of an evening. We'd gazed, too, when it had shown birds fluttering around. But this machine was larger and flatter.

I heard the Persian cat strike another key. As I watched, the screen, which had been dead, suddenly came to life and lit up. And then the miracle happened—I saw my brothers! There they were on this other screen in front of me. They were both guzzling away at laden plates, and they were surrounded by tins of cat food. I knew at once it was Peter and Pipkin—they were unmistakable with their markings that were exactly the same as mine.

I mewed a great cry of surprise and delight. I squatted on my hind legs and tried to touch my brothers with my forepaws—but the glass was hard and unyielding. I couldn't get through to them. They were only a moving picture, and yet they were real. They were somewhere in this mysterious box. Somewhere behind the glass where I couldn't reach them.

The Persian cat lowered himself carefully from his chair and sat beside me.

'Are those your brothers?' he enquired. He was purring with satisfaction at his own cleverness, which, I realised later, he'd only achieved by a lucky chance.

I answered his question with a nod of assent. I couldn't take my eyes off my dear siblings, who, having finished their meal, were beginning to wash themselves just as Fozzy had taught us. But even as I watched, they disappeared from view. A man came on and said something. There was no sound,

only writing which I couldn't read. I dashed behind the magic box to investigate this mystery, but there was nothing there. I couldn't understand any of it.

'There,' said the Persian cat, smug with self-satisfaction. 'I told you I'd find them for you.'

I turned away from the screen. It was no longer interesting. 'But where *are* they?' I persisted.

The Persian's flat grey face remained quite impassive. 'I've shown you—they were there.'

'But where's "there"?' I was getting desperate, and my miaows had turned to a high squeak.

'Well, you saw where they were. Inside my master's magic box. And perfectly happy with all those nice tins of cat food. I rather fancy trying it myself. I shall have to see if I can get my servants to buy me some. I wonder what flavours there are?'

I had sniffed all round the box and found nothing. I felt hopeless and frustrated. I'd seen my brothers but I'd still no idea how to get to them. For all I knew they were being held hostage. Probably they'd been bribed with all those tins—I knew how greedy they both were. They'd do anything for food, those two.

The conceited cat was now sitting on the thick cream-coloured carpet, giving his long fur a perfunctory lick.

'You'd better scarper now, kitten. A human will be coming to groom me soon.'

I stared at him. I couldn't believe this was the only help I was going to get after bringing him his desired mouse.

'I said you'd better leave now.' The big cat was rolling on his back, dangling all his paws in the air. 'And a word of thanks wouldn't come amiss,' he hissed in my ear.

I was so bitterly disappointed I could have cried out. All I could manage was a muttered, 'Thank you.'

I made my way down the long corridor and across the black-and-white tiles of the hall. The big clock was still ticking away the minutes. I pushed open the cat flap and was met by the cold winter air.

I had no idea what to do next.

Chapter 6

Peter and Pipkin Take Up the Tale

When the strange man put us both in his dark box at Mrs Lovejoy's that evening, we were terrified. We mewed with fright, calling out to Fozzy, our mother, and our sister Polly. We'd never been separated from them before. We huddled together (we were pretty squashed anyway) and nuzzled each other's tabby fur for comfort. The swaying of the box made us feel sick.

The man had parked his car a little way away from Mrs Lovejoy's house. We heard the car door being opened, and then we felt the box in which we were imprisoned being placed on the front seat. After a few minutes the car began to move. We believed we would never see our loved ones again.

The drive went on for hours and hours. We thought it was never going to end. But at long last the car stopped and our box was lifted out. More swaying and sickness. We then realised we'd been taken into some large building. We could hear people talking and walking about. Then the box was dumped down on a wooden surface.

We heard the man say in a commanding voice, 'Get Jilly for me. I've got 'em. Just the ticket—as alike as two peas. Found 'em right out in the country. Jilly will look after 'em—she'll report back to me.'

We were left alone in the dark carrying box, and the minutes slipped by. We'd no idea what our fate was going to be. Why did the man want us so much? What was he going to do with us?

Footsteps, and then another quick interchange of human conversation. A cool girl's voice said, 'The Maestro has left them here for you, Jilly.'

And then another slightly higher girl's voice replying, 'I can't wait to see what he's found. Where am I to take them?'

'Dressing room 28.'

What did that mean? Again the box was lifted up and we were swinging in mid-air. Luckily the ride wasn't very long this time. Another door opened and closed. So we were to be shut in. We huddled together as the lid of the box was opened.

'Oh, aren't you little darlings?' said the girl, who we supposed was Jilly. She lifted us out quite gently, but the floor on which she placed us was bare and slippery. We skidded about for a few minutes while Jilly watched us intently. We looked about for some food, but there wasn't any.

Then Jilly picked us up and placed us on a strange table. That surface was slippery, too. It was backed by a huge mirror completely surrounded by light bulbs. Jilly suddenly turned these on.

'All the better to see you with,' she said.

But we were dazzled, and we both closed our eyes.

Jilly stroked us gently, one of us with each hand. We managed a few hesitant purrs. We were both anxious to please in these strange surroundings. Perhaps, if we behaved very well, we would be returned to Mrs Lovejoy and our dear mother Fozzy.

Jilly seemed to like the look of us. She crooned away, 'Aren't you little sweeties? And complete lookalikes. Just what the company wanted. So clever of the Maestro to find you. Brilliant. Provided, of course'— and here her voice took on a sterner, almost scolding tone—'you do exactly as you're told. Now, are you biddable kittens?'

We didn't know what 'biddable' meant. We only knew that we were hungry. We both began to squeak.

Luckily the brown-haired girl, who was wearing jeans and a T-shirt, got the message almost at once.

'Oh dear, I bet nobody's thought about you needing to be fed. I'll have to go and see what I can get from the canteen. Tomorrow I'll organise some proper cat food for you. Stay here, boys, and be good.'

We didn't have much option about what we could do. Brushing back her curly hair, she lowered us to the slippery floor once again. She closed the door very firmly behind her. The only window in the stuffy little room was high up on the bare cream wall.

After she'd gone we inspected the room. There wasn't much to discover. There were some very hot pipes that nearly burnt our sensitive noses, an uncomfortable upright chair by the strange table, a very old sofa and a rather decrepit arm-chair.

We were trying to snuggle up on that when Jilly returned.

'Guys, I'm sorry, this is the best I can do for you tonight. No one seems to have thought of feeding you or looking after you. It was all "Get some kittens", "We need two kittens!" I just hope this'll keep you going.'

She produced a great deal of smoked salmon (that had been taken out of sandwiches) and a carton of milk. She laid the salmon out on some newspaper. We jumped down and began to gulp our meal. It was delicious, but very strong. Jilly poured some of the milk into a saucer for us. At home we only had water to drink, so at first we lapped tentatively. Then we decided we liked it—it was a pleasant change. (Though actually it didn't agree with us and our insides got thoroughly upset.)

Jilly watched us devouring the salmon until there wasn't a scrap left.

'Well, it's night-night, kits, sleep tight. You'll have to sleep in your box tonight—I'll rig up a proper bed for you tomorrow.'

She turned the box on its side so that we could crawl onto the rather pathetic bit of blanket inside it.

'I'm off now—I'm on overtime already.'

She turned off the lights, closed the door and left us alone in this strange, rather stuffy room.

Some light was coming in from the tiny window high up

on the wall. We explored the room to see if there was any means of escape. We decided there wasn't, so we curled up together on the old armchair. We certainly weren't going to pass the night in the box in which we'd been held captive.

We slept fitfully, nose to tail, snuggling into each other's fur. We were so glad of each other's company.

It was quite late in the morning when Jilly woke us, switching on all the electric lights. In this place you needed them all the time, we discovered. No daylight was allowed in.

'Well, how are my kits this morning? At least I've bought you some proper cat food. I stopped at the pet shop on my way to work. You should be getting it for free, but I don't know where they're keeping it.'

She produced some packets of a kind of cat food that we didn't know. Once again she put it on newspaper—it didn't occur to her to put it in dishes for us. And as she hadn't given a thought to our toilet training either, we'd used the newspaper the night before.

We both sniffed suspiciously at the new food—it didn't smell very good. But finally hunger overcame us and we ate some of it.

'Come on, boys,' urged Jilly. 'You must like it. Soon you're going to have to eat lots of it.'

But we'd had enough. We'd also drunk a little of the milk (which still didn't agree with us).

Jilly said, 'Look what else I bought . . .' She produced a cat brush and comb. 'Must remember to get all this off expenses,' she added. We didn't know what she was talking about.

52

In turn, she lifted each of us onto the table with the mirror and all the lights. She gave us a thorough grooming, until our black-and-tabby coats shone like silk.

'Got to look your best, you know. You're going to be stars.'

Those twinkly things in the sky that Mrs Lovejoy had shown us? That remark filled us with terror. So were we going to be killed after all? So that our little dead selves would go up into the sky and become stars?

As soon as we were back on the floor again we scuttled for safety under the sofa. It was a tight squeeze—we are both quite plump. But we lay there breathing heavily, expecting we knew not what.

What did happen was that Jilly gave several rather futile cries of, 'Kittens, come out of there!' And of course we didn't respond. So the girl lay on the floor and pulled us out none too gently. Then she put us both in the travelling box and shut the lid firmly.

We only knew that we were being carried about the building. We heard various humans saying, 'Hi, Jilly,' and one or two, 'Are those the kittens?'

Our guardian went into a small enclosed space that seemed to be full of people all crowded together.

A man said, 'Which floor, Jilly?' and she answered, 'Third.'

Then there was the most extraordinary sensation—we seemed to be flying upwards. Were we indeed going to those stars she'd mentioned? Our tummies, already overfull with the cat food, seemed to plummet down. The metal cage (for

53

that was what we'd decided it was) shuddered to a halt. We heard sliding doors opening.

'Level Three,' said a voice, and to our relief Jilly stepped out onto solid flooring.

But where on earth had she brought us? There seemed to be lots of people shouting instructions to each other:

'Lights!'

'Dim it!'

'Want an amber, Ron?'

'Zoom in a bit, Derek.'

It was all a wild cacophony to our ears. We did so want Mrs Lovejoy to be there with her calm voice, telling us everything was going to be all right.

Jilly had put our box down on a chair now, and she was sitting beside us. Once or twice she opened the lid and scratched our heads or behind our ears, but it wasn't very comforting.

At last she took us out of confinement and held us on her lap. We struggled at first but she gripped us both firmly. The material of her jeans was hard and scratchy. We decided we'd better give in and stay still, at least for a while.

Suddenly the hubbub quietened. All the people (and there were so many) seemed to be standing to attention. Then the big man who had taken us away came striding towards us. He stepped carefully over all the things like rubber snakes that littered the floor. He loomed over Jilly and looked down at us. We crouched fearfully on her lap.

'Nice little things, aren't they? Real bit of luck finding

them. I was in Milchester over the weekend, visiting my mother. Went into a shop for some ciggies. Saw this advert—and there they were—bingo! Just right for the job, eh?'

He gave us what was meant to be a playful chuck under the chin, but actually it hurt.

We noticed the man had strange things over his ears, with a wire hanging from them. They couldn't be earmuffs—he couldn't be cold! This place—whatever it was—and we'd heard some of the men refer to it as a 'studio'—was boiling hot. We wished someone could unzip our fur.

The mysterious man—who all the people addressed as 'Hal'—seemed to be talking to someone who wasn't there. He had lots of other wires coming from other parts of his body. He seemed to be getting messages from nowhere.

Finally he spoke to us, or rather Jilly.

'Baz says let's get started. This commercial's got to be out and showing before the Christmas season starts if it's to make an impact. Time's money, as we all know, so let's go—'

'Where d'you want them?' Jilly was already standing up, one of us grasped firmly in either hand.

By way of answer, Hal, the mystery man, led the way to a brightly lit space where a table with a blue-checked cloth had been laid out. In the centre of the table was a pyramid of tins of the cat food we'd had for breakfast (and hadn't liked very much. We preferred the brand Mrs Lovejoy had given us at home). On either side of the pyramid was a dish of the stuff, smelling rather nasty.

Jilly placed us each in front of one of the dishes, saying, 'Stay.'

'Good, let's have a rehearsal.' Hal sped away. He moved very nimbly for such a big man, stepping neatly over all the rubber snakes. (We learnt, much later, they were called 'cables'.)

From somewhere far away he shouted, 'Action!'

The bright space became a hundred times brighter. A large black box that moved began to whirr. It had a red light on the front of it that winked as it came towards us. We both sniffed the contents of our saucers disdainfully—it really did smell rather horrible. So we both turned our backs on the food and set out to see how we could rejoin each other. But the pyramid of tins was in the way.

'Cut,' came the voice of the strange man from far away. Some of the big suns around us were dimmed, but it was still unbearably hot.

Hal arrived back at the table and jabbed a forefinger at Jilly, who'd been standing by.

'That was hopeless,' he snarled. 'Baz says make them eat.'

'I can't *make* them do anything,' replied the girl, who was now fondling us. She seemed to be on our side.

'They're just not hungry, Hal,' said a man standing beside one of the suns with its long black legs. He adjusted it so that still more heat poured onto our fur.

'Did you feed them this morning?' Our tormentor was accusing Jilly.

'Well . . . er . . . yes . . . I never thought . . .'

For Pete's sake!' (Peter pricked up his ears at the mention of his name.) 'It's obvious they've got to be starving to do it. But we must get it in the can. Come on, keep trying.'

And so it went on, hour after terrible hour. The cry would go up, 'Lights, camera, action.' And the heat and light would increase and the whirring grew louder and Jilly tried to tempt us with bits of the nasty food on the end of her finger.

But for us the end came when the horrible man came to the table and forcibly pushed our noses into the disgusting stuff. Until that moment we'd taken it all pretty placidly, lying on our sides, panting with the heat, between 'takes', as these periods of violent activity seemed to be called. But to have our noses rubbed in it—that really was too much. Of course we weren't going to eat the revolting mess.

As the cry of 'action' came once again we both had the same thought—to rejoin each other. We charged at the pyramid of tins at the same moment. With our combined weights coming from either side, we managed to send the tins flying in all directions.

Thankfully we rubbed noses—it was good to be together again. Then we both leapt off the table, dragging the table-cloth with us, which dislodged further tins. We slithered between people's legs as agitated hands tried to grab us. We skipped over the snaky coils and dodged all the strange objects that filled the place.

We were determined we wouldn't be caught.

Chapter 7

Peter and Pipkin Continue Their Story

But of course they did get us in the end—it was twenty people against two small kittens in an enclosed space. Many hands grabbed us roughly and hauled us out from our hiding place. We'd been sheltering behind some huge black boxes. It had been a squeeze to get into the space, but for a short while we'd felt safe. Now it was all over.

'Here y'are. The little varmints.'

The man who'd found us held us close against his T-shirt, which had something written on it we couldn't read.

'Can't go blaming the kits. They just wasn't hungry.'

All the men, and there were a few women too, were standing round in a circle staring at us.

'They're cute though, aren't they? I bet they'll sell it.' This was from a lady in trousers.

At that moment our mysterious snatcher, Hal, elbowed his way into the group. He was closely followed by Jilly. He grabbed us both and held us high so that we were close to his piercing black eyes and his black beard (which felt prickly).

Our back legs were dangling helplessly—we were very uncomfortable.

'You little—' and Hal used a word we'd never heard before.

We became thoroughly alarmed when our unpleasant tormentor continued, 'And you've both cost us an extra day's shooting.'

We tried to look at each other—were we, after all, going to be shot? We reached out our white-tipped front paws and tried to scratch the goatee beard in front of us. Hal hurriedly handed us to Jilly.

'Take 'em away. Don't let me have a sight of them till tomorrow. And of course, NO FOOD. You must see they don't get *anything*. Those kittens have to be starving in the morning or this'll be the last thing I'll do.'

The girl—we'd heard people calling her his PA, but we didn't know what that meant—packed us into the travelling box again. There was another of those awful journeys. We knew we went down in the metal-box thing again—we both had that dreadful sinking feeling. We heard the doors clang behind us, and soon Jilly was lifting us out into the little room where we'd spent the previous night.

'Night-night, kits. Be good. No food tonight, but what a feast you're going to get tomorrow.'

She laid some sheets of newspaper on the floor, presumably for our toilet, since we weren't getting anything to eat. Then she switched off the lights and closed the door behind her.

We were both so unhappy and miserable. Our tummies

60

were rumbling for want of some nice food, and we were tired out after our exhausting day in 'the studio'.

Then, with horror, we realised that Jilly hadn't left us anything to drink, not even water (which we much preferred to milk anyway). Our tongues were sticking to the roofs of our mouths for want of moisture. We were panting with thirst. The great thought came to us both at the same moment. We jumped—only it was more of a scramble—onto the back of the sofa. From there it was a comparatively short leap into the white enamel washbasin. And, oh glory, one of the taps was dripping strongly. Even so, it took us a long time to satisfy our thirst. We politely took it in turns to hold our heads under the tap to catch the precious drops. But at last we'd had enough, and we jumped back down to the floor.

By mutual consent we went and sat on the newspaper to consider our position. What we didn't know was that it was the local paper Hal's mother had posted to her son. (She thought he wanted to keep up with the news of his home town—which he didn't. He'd hastily passed the newspaper on to Jilly for our use.) And we were sitting right on top of the agonised advertisement Mrs Lovejoy had inserted about our disappearance. It said: *'TAKEN AWAY: two tabby kittens. White bibs and white tips to paws. Identical. If you've seen them or know where they are, please contact . . .'*

If only we'd been able to read . . . though we'd have had no way of letting her know our whereabouts. We longed to tell Fozzy all about the strange things that were happening to us.

We passed the night fitfully—we were so glad of each

other's company. But above all else, we were so hungry. Our tummies rumbled uncontrollably, we'd never wanted food so much. And, feeling starved, we grew colder, and huddled into each other's fur.

At long last the lights were switched on and Jilly bounced into the room.

'No breakfast for you chaps, you're going to have to perform!'

What was to 'perform'? It sounded sinister to us. Jilly skipped about collecting the scattered sheets of newspaper. She didn't look at them—she didn't see Mrs L.'s heart-rending plea for news of us. But she made 'Tch, tch' noises when she saw the arms of the sofa. In desperation, during the night, we'd had a good chew there. We'd also managed a fair amount of clawing on the faded chintz.

'I've brought you some water.' The girl produced a saucer and a small bottle.

'Pity you didn't think of that last night, and lucky we found our own supply,' we thought privately. But we were feeling so weak we lapped dutifully.

Then it was into the box again and an uncomfortable ride up to that peculiar place, 'the studio'. Jilly unpacked us at once, and proceeded to brush and comb us very carefully. We were so weak with hunger we stayed quite still on her lap.

There were all the strange people again, only this morning they made quite a fuss of us, especially the female ones.

'Aren't they little darlings?' they cooed, scratching us under the chin, just where we liked it.

Someone muttered, 'Them kittens yesterday—they got us an extra day's work. We owe 'em one. Make it good, lads!'

Then Hal, the mystery man, arrived and tweaked our tails, which we didn't like.

'Nice and hungry, are we? Get 'em set up, Jilly. Ready for a del-ic-ious breakfast, eh?'

The very way he said it made it sound sinister.

So Jilly popped us onto the blue-checked tablecloth once more. The pyramid of tins had been rebuilt. And there were two saucers of the once-despised cat food. But—heads down—we immediately started guzzling. And boy, did it taste great after our long fast!

'Stop 'em! Stop 'em!' screamed our top man. 'I'm not ready to shoot. Jilly, you must hold 'em till the very last moment.'

Jilly grabbed us, and we wriggled. We'd seen food and we wanted it—fast.

We had to wait for what seemed like ages. At last the call came for 'Lights!' and the brightness and the heat dazzled and frazzled us. Finally it was 'Action!' and Jilly put us back on the table. In no time at all we were gobbling the food, heads down and tails erect, quite unaware of the black machine with the red winking eye that zoomed in so close to us.

There was a cry of 'Cut!' and Jilly swiftly removed us from the half-eaten saucers. She held us for some time, and nothing seemed to be happening.

Then the Big Man reappeared.

'Well done, everybody,' he said. 'That was perfect. Purr-fect.' He seemed pleased with his own pun, and even gave us

64

a little stroke. 'We'll just go for one more take. Places everyone. Jilly, don't put them on the table till the very last minute. They're still hungry, aren't they?'

And then we were supposed to go through it all again. Only this time we weren't hungry—we'd had quite enough of the nasty food to stem our appetites. So of course we turned our noses up when we were faced with the saucers. There were groans from everyone in the studio.

Until Jilly said suddenly, 'I've had a brainwave. Here— somebody hold the kittens for me.'

Several eager hands grabbed us—we were certainly popular. After a short while Jilly arrived back in the studio. She was panting for breath, but she was clutching a plate.

'It's salmon from the sandwiches. This is what they really like,' she announced breathlessly. 'Let's try the take again.'

So once more, on the cry of 'Action!', we were placed in front of the saucers. Only this time they were full of this delicious salmon. 'The right stuff for kittens,' we thought. So we licked our saucers bare and then carefully cleaned our faces and whiskers with our white-tipped paws, just as Fozzy had taught us.

The cry of 'Cut!' came from a long way off, and there was silence. Then, suddenly, all the people in this strange place started clapping. At first we were startled by the noise, and then we realised they were applauding *us*. Secretly we felt rather pleased with ourselves. Except that we hadn't done anything—we'd only gulped down some rather tasty salmon.

But all these people came crowding round the table and

stroking us, and saying how wonderful we'd been, and that we were 'naturals', whatever that meant. So we both felt a bit embarrassed, but ever so much better with some good food inside us.

With our renewed energy we decided it was time to play. At the same moment, from either side, we head-butted the pile of tins. It was a very satisfactory feeling seeing them— once again—go flying in all directions.

The strange Hal appeared. His normally pale face had a reddish tinge and beads of sweat were dripping into his black goatee beard. But he did seem pleased.

'Well done,' he said. 'Well done, everyone. Couldn't have been better. We got it all. Magical. Ten out of ten. And when they sat and washed their faces—perfect. Purr-fect, you little beggars.'

We'd been recaptured, and Jilly was holding us once more, but we were struggling in her arms. We definitely felt more active.

Then she said quietly, 'What happens to them now?'

Hal was mopping his face with a very large, very clean white handkerchief.

'Oh, I'll send 'em back to Mrs Whatshername,' he mumbled. 'Oh, damn. I've forgotten her name. And address.'

Jilly raised her eyebrows. 'So, they've made the commercial, but what becomes of them?'

Chapter 8

In Which I Get Nabbed by the Law, and Enter a Great Building

Hi, this is, Polly, continuing my side of the story. After I left the rich cat's house I felt so defeated I spent many hours sitting in the cold, dank garden. True, I had seen a moving picture of my brothers. They'd seemed to be eating heartily, and I knew that would keep them happy and content. But where exactly were they? What was this 'moving picture' I'd seen? And above everything else, how could I reach them?

It was long after lunchtime and the air was getting colder. I sniffed, twitching my long white whiskers: I could smell that frost, or possibly even snow, was coming that night. Eventually I made my way away from the garden towards the busy streets of the town. There seemed to be a great many people about. I didn't know it was Christmas shoppers crowding the pavements. Carrier bags banged against me, and small children put out sticky fingers to touch my coat. (My fur, once Mrs Lovejoy's pride and joy, had become dull and dusty now I was living like an outlaw.) But I pressed on, avoiding pram wheels and scooters as best I could.

Then I came to a shop with a very large plate-glass window. Feeling tired and hungry, I sat down on the pavement. What I saw made me gasp with astonishment. The window was filled with a line of boxes, and each one displayed a moving, flickering picture. All the pictures were the same—I moved along the line—and they were of my brothers! I knew I wasn't mistaken—there were Peter and Pipkin, heartily tucking into saucers of food. And when they'd finished eating they sat down and licked their forepaws and cleaned their faces, just as Fozzy had taught us. I couldn't believe my own eyes. There they were, inside the boxes, just as they had been in the posh cat's house.

I stood on my hind legs and pushed my nose and forepaws against the shop window. The glass was hard and unyielding. As I watched, the pictures of my brothers disappeared. In their place came a bright young man holding a wooden thing with strings which he proceeded to play. I sat back on my haunches. I was completely baffled. *Where were they?* Were they inside these magic boxes? Mrs Lovejoy had one in her front room and my brothers weren't on that . . . I couldn't understand how they could be behind glass and in several different places. If only I could find them and hear what was happening to them. I needed an explanation for these mysterious sightings.

Eventually hunger drove me away from the curious boxes. I came to a shop where the smell of fish was very strong. And

71

joy of joys, someone had thrown down a half-consumed meal in some newspaper by the door. I gobbled the lot, and, in my extreme hunger, I dropped my guard for a moment. And that moment was my undoing: strong hands gripped me and I was lifted against a navy serge uniform.

'Now what've we got here? You're a pretty kitten, aren't you?'

I tried spitting in the policeman's red face, and wriggled as much as I could. But he continued to hold me in a vice-like grip.

'You must be a stray,' he continued. 'Wandering the streets on Christmas Eve an' goin' for them fish an' chips like you'd never had a decent meal. Bet my life someone's missing you. You'd best come along wiv me to the station and see if anyone's been askin' after you. Here we go. Station's just up here by the Cathedral.'

Although I fought against him every inch of the way, the stout policeman carried me to the police station. I was spitting with fury—hadn't I seen my brothers with my own eyes? They must be somewhere very close, I must be nearly at the end of my quest. And, rightly as it turned out, I guessed Mrs Lovejoy would have reported me missing to the police. Once at the station I would be returned to her—and never discover what had happened to Peter and Pipkin.

I was still trying to scratch my way to freedom when we reached the police station.

'Whatcher got there, Bob?' asked the sergeant sitting behind the counter. He put his mug of tea down carefully.

'Beautiful little kitten, if it weren't so vexed at me pickin' it up. Someone's pride and joy, I'll be bound. Found wanderin' all alone in Cathedral Street. Anyone been askin' for it?'

'Lady called in half an hour ago. Lost a tabby kitten with white markings. Bet it's this one, Bob. I'll just get her number and give her a ring. Hang on a sec . . .' He turned away from the desk to consult some papers.

'Hanging on' was just what Bob was doing. He'd put me on the counter, but his huge hands gripped me. And then the miracle happened: the policeman sneezed—long and loudly. He loosened his grip as both his hands moved instinctively to find the handkerchief in his trouser pocket.

I seized my chance and jumped to the floor, overturning the sergeant's cuppa as I went. I dashed for the door, and once again my luck held. A young couple were coming in, and I managed to squeeze between their legs. I heard cries of 'Catch that kitten!' But I'd got away.

Now I needed time to think. My heart was beating so fast—I was gasping for breath. I followed a few people who were turning in from the street under an old grey stone arch. In front of us was a lovely stretch of grass—it felt so soft under my tired paws. Beyond the grass was a huge towering red stone building. There were stone people all over the front (I wondered if they were previous owners?) and three huge doors, all of them wide open. Light streamed out from the building, and coming from a distance I heard music unlike any I'd heard before. 'Whoever lives in a house as big as this?' I wondered. But they seemed welcoming with their open

73

doors. And then, from somewhere high up in one of the three towers, bells began to ring.

'Come,' they seemed to say. 'Come. Come in.' I sensed there would be a welcome for a tired kitten inside this great building. For now I was worn out. I was exhausted by all my adventures and the hopelessness of my quest for my brothers. All I wanted was to be very quiet and sleep. I tiptoed into the building. My nose twitched at the strange smells, and the stone and marble slabs were cool under my pads.

There were rows and rows of wooden seats all neatly arranged. It seemed that the owner was expecting many guests. The chairs looked very hard to me, but in front of each was a cushiony thing, as if the occupant of each chair would have a kitten with them, too.

I chose a blue one at the foot of a huge pillar about halfway down the long building. I curled up on it, tucking my tail in neatly and putting one paw over my eyes. Within seconds I was fast asleep. And while I slept I dreamt. My dream was of Peter and Pipkin being chased by the mysterious man who'd taken them away—not alive and well, as I'd seen them on the magic boxes.

But my sleep didn't last very long. I was woken by more people coming into the building. They were all clutching white papers, and they sat on chairs about the building. An elderly couple came into my row, and I thought it was time to move before they spotted me.

I walked towards the centre of this mysterious building, and the music grew louder. At the very heart of the building there was a table covered in a red and gold cloth. It was set with silver and gold dishes and two tall candlesticks. Someone was definitely expected. Everywhere the lights flickered. I could hear more and more people coming into the building, and I moved away to the right. And there I found the perfect hiding place. It was a large box, just the right size. Had they been expecting a kitten? It was a couple of feet off the ground, with sturdy legs, an easy jump for me. Inside the box was thickly lined with hay and straw. I burrowed into it. The hay was warm and comforting and I felt safe at last. There were some little wooden figures in the box, but they didn't disturb me and I didn't disturb them. There was singing in the great place, but it sounded very far away. I slept and slept.

When at last the singing had finished a number of people came and stood in front of my box. I only opened one eye. I felt quite safe. I was completely hidden in the straw and no one saw me. Even when a few of them came with lighted candles they didn't spot me. They drifted away, still holding their flickering tapers. At last the whole place grew silent. I heard the large doors slam shut, far away. Then I fell into an exhausted sleep from which it seemed nothing would wake me.

I suppose it must have been some time in the very early morning when I came to. Although I'd been so warm nestling in the hay, I suddenly felt cold. I uncurled myself and had a good stretch. Then I realised I badly needed to pee, so I jumped down from my box, taking care not to knock over any of the wooden figures. I set off down the long stone aisle looking for somewhere to relieve myself There didn't seem to be anywhere suitable. Hadn't the owner of this lofty building, that seemed so welcoming to small kittens, made any provision for this natural act?

And then it happened: suddenly, without any warning, there was a loud and hideous noise of shrill alarm bells ringing all over the building. Paralysed with terror and deafened by the noise, I crouched at the base of a great stone pillar. I was frozen with fear, and quite forgot about my other need.

Then I heard a little door behind me, that I hadn't noticed, being opened and shut again. And suddenly—oh, the relief— the horrible din ceased. Still I crouched there as a small blob of light, followed by footsteps, came towards me. The light was shining directly into my eyes.

A voice, for it was a man carrying a torch, called out sharply, 'Who's there?' And then, more kindly, 'Why, it's only a kitten.' He stopped and picked me up. His hands were firm but gentle, and for the first time in a long while I felt safe with a human being. I knew this man would help me in some way. He caressed me tenderly. I almost felt like purring.

'What's a young kitten like you doing alone in the Cathedral? You must have walked through the alarm beam, that's what you've been and done. Gave me the fright of my life, I can tell you. Set all the alarm bells off, that's what you did. *And* the one in my house. Got me out of bed, you did, seeing as how I'm responsible for the security in here.'

77

And all the time he talked he was stroking me gently. By now I was really purring.

'And you chose this morning of all mornings, didn't you? Christmas Day. I don't suppose you knew that, did you, young kit? And it wouldn't mean much to you, anyroads. But we've a busy day in front of us here—all the services. There'll be lots of people—they do like to sing the carols—bless 'em.'

He had now reached the little side door, which he opened. There was a blast of cold air from outside, and I saw there was white stuff all over the ground.

'Seasonal snow, too. That's what people like—a white Christmas. You're a real Christmas kitten, you are.'

He was walking towards a small house very near to the Cathedral, as I now knew the great building that had sheltered me, was called. He opened the front door with a little brass key and once more I was in the warmth.

The man, who said he was a verger (but I didn't know what that meant), fussed over me almost as Mrs Lovejoy would have done. He seemed to realise my plight, for he made a pile of newspaper in a secluded corner where I could relieve myself. That duty attended to, and after I'd had a quick wash and brush up, he plied me with delicate morsels of something he called turkey. Anyway, it was delicious, and I was *so* hungry.

'Lucky I cooked the bird yesterday,' murmured the man. 'But then I always do, what with us being so busy on the Day.'

Then he put a saucer of milk before me. It's funny how

humans always think we want milk—I would have much preferred water. But the man was being so kind I lapped dutifully.

'Must get a move on,' said the man, and he took off the mackintosh he'd been wearing over his pyjamas and changed from them into a smart dark suit. Over that he put a wide black coat with velvet facings and long pointed sleeves.

'My uniform,' he explained. 'I lead the processions of the choir and clergy around the Cathedral. Which reminds me, Christmas kitten, I'll have to take you over to the Deanery later in the day—once all the services are finished. Me finding you in the Cathedral makes you the Dean's property. I'm sure he'll find out where you've strayed from and who owns you.'

He made me a comfortable bed on a blanket in front of the gas fire, with another plate of chopped-up turkey in case I felt hungry again.

'Be good, kitten,' he said as he closed the door. 'I'm off to early service.'

Then he left me alone with my thoughts.

Chapter 9

What's going to Happen to Peter and Pipkin?

Some weeks earlier, back in the studio many miles from the cathedral town of Milchester, Jilly repeated her question: 'What are we going to do with them?' (Meaning us, Peter and Pipkin.)

We'd just done what these strange people called 'Making a TV commercial'. All we knew was that we'd had too much to eat and were feeling rather sick as a result. Hal, the strange man who'd taken us from Mrs Lovejoy that evening that seemed so long ago, tapped the side of his head.

'How could I be so stupid as to lose that woman's address?'

Although we were afraid of him, we thought to lose our home address was pretty foolish. We guessed Jilly felt the same, though as he was her boss she couldn't say so. Instead she stroked us. Replete after our large meal, we were pretending to be asleep.

'The RSPCA might take them,' she suggested helpfully. There was a pause, and then she said suddenly, 'I've had a brainwave!' She was so excited she nearly tipped us off her lap. 'What about Paul's show? He often has unwanted animals on that—he asks people to offer them good homes.'

'Jilly, you're a star!' The director thumped her on the back, and once more we were nearly dislodged. 'Paul's got a special show on Christmas afternoon. The commercial will've been on for a long time by then, and the kittens will be famous. People will be falling over themselves to give them homes— we'll call them "The Christmas Kittens". It'll be wonderful publicity for us and for Paul.'

'I'll take them home and look after them—as long as it's only until then. Mum won't mind if they're not staying permanently.'

'It gets better and better. I'll get Paul on the blower and fix it all up. You'll take care of the little blighters and bring them in for the show?'

'Will do, Boss.'

With another hearty slap on her back, Hal left Jilly to pack us into the travelling box once more. Then off we went to Jilly's home. Most of what had been said had gone over our heads, and we didn't know what was going to happen to us— only that we were on the move once more.

We could feel Jilly, who was really quite kind to us, stowing our box into what we took was her car. It was only a short drive, but it was a rattly one—our box bounced about and we felt sicker than ever.

But Jilly braked suddenly and announced, 'Here we are, kits.'

She carried our box into what we discovered later was a

small, rather poky flat. She opened the lid and an old lady with wispy grey hair peered down at us.

'Mother, meet the television kittens!' Jilly explained about us going onto this other show to find a home. We didn't know what she was talking about.

Her mother lifted us out of the box, quite gently.

'Well,' she said quietly. 'As long as it's only for a while. I've always said I won't have animals in this flat. It's too small for pets.'

Jilly was hugging us now. I really think she would have liked to keep us permanently.

'It's not for too long, Mum, I promise. Only 'till Christmas.'

The time we spent with Jilly and her mother passed pleasantly enough. But we began to be alarmed on the morning Jilly woke us up very early. (She'd made a comfy bed for us to sleep in—a cut-down cardboard box lined with a blanket.) We saw that the tiny flat had been decorated with branches of spiky green leaves with red berries. We tried to eat some of these and got a good telling off. Actually they didn't taste at all nice and we both spat them out.

Jilly and her mother exchanged presents wrapped in sheets of crinkly, bright-coloured paper. We had a few good games diving through these while they were still lying on the floor. (Which wasn't for very long. Jilly's mother was a very tidy person.)

After we'd had our breakfast, Jilly gave us a thorough brush-and-comb grooming.

'Got to look your best, kits,' she said. 'Your whole future depends on the show today.'

We wondered what she meant, and when we were packed into the travelling box again, where we were going this time.

We didn't have to wait long to find out. It was only another short bumpy ride in Jilly's old car before we were back at the TV studio again. And how we hated it! The dust, the smells, the hot lights, and all the people milling around us . . .

The studio was laid out rather differently now. There was the stage/living-room area where we had been with the tins of cat food. But now, in front of that, there were rows and rows of empty seats.

Jilly tried taking us out of the box, but as soon as we realised where we were, we fought and scratched at her and anyone else who came near us.

'Best keep the little blighters shut up,' said an unfriendly man who was in charge of the black box with the winking red eye. We had learnt it was called 'the camera'. Actually, there were several about the studio that would come at us from different angles. Everyone treated them with great respect, but we found them frightening.

'Better take them somewhere quiet, Jilly,' said a woman holding a clipboard. She had cropped hair and had wires hanging all over her. In her authoritative voice she continued, 'We shan't want them till this afternoon.'

Jilly did what the woman suggested. She found a peaceful corner in somewhere she called 'the canteen'. A big stout woman in a white overall and a cap which hid all her hair produced some tasty snacks for us. We'd been unpacked yet again.

'Aren't they little darlings?' said the fat woman. 'My shift finishes at two. I always watch Paul's show. I've got a good mind to put in an offer for them myself. Two kittens would be handy where I live—keep down the mice.'

We took no notice of this, and, feeling refreshed, we had a great game of catch-as-catch-can round all the table and chair legs. Then the room began to fill up with people. They stood in a long line to collect trays laden with steaming plates of food, which smelt good. Our nostrils twitched, and Jilly picked us up.

The fat lady brought us another delicious meal. Soon we were so full we fell asleep on Jilly's lap. We each opened an eye when people came and said, 'Are those the kittens that are going to be on Paul's show?' and, 'Oh, it's the Cat Food Commercial Kittens! Aren't they cute?'

Everyone was interested in us.

The canteen emptied again and we went on snoozing comfortably on Jilly's lap. At last a boy in black leather, who had things over his ears which seemed to tell him what to do, came and said, 'Miss Emmerson, kittens to the studio now, please.'

So we went back to the horrid place again. Jilly tiptoed in and sat on a chair by the wall. She took us out of the box and held us tightly on her knees. It was very dark, and there was a terrible hush over the whole place. But there was a great noise coming from the rows and rows of seats that had been empty. Now they were filled with people who were laughing and clapping. They seemed to be watching a man who was in the living-room area facing them.

This man did all sorts of strange things, and the people in front kept applauding him. We had to stretch our necks to see all that was going on. The man was middle-aged and he had silvery grey hair and wore spectacles. He talked very excitedly and waved his arms around. All the people sitting in the seats seemed to love him.

'And now folks,' said Paul, making another big circle with his arms, 'it's yer favourite bit of the show—the bit yer like the best. Folks—it's Find-A-Pet-A-Home time.'

There was a huge burst of clapping from the people sitting out front, which startled us. Paul spoke again, overriding the applause.

'Today, being Christmas, we have something extra special for you. Not just one pet, but two! And I must emphasise they must be homed together. They're brothers and we're not splitting 'em up. And, as I always say, don't ring in unless you're really serious and can truly offer them a good home. You know the number to call. Jilly—bring 'em on. Folks—I give you the Cat Food Commerical Kittens! Yes, it's really them—as seen on TV. And they're looking for a good home with someone out there watching at this very moment. Now—who's going to be the lucky new owner of the famous twins?'

Jilly had placed us on the desk in front of Paul. Several of

the big black boxes with winking red eyes zoomed in very close to us, but Jilly was standing nearby. We vaguely wondered if our beloved Mrs Lovejoy would get this message. How wonderful it would be if she claimed us, and we went back to where we felt we belonged. But it seemed more likely we would go to some complete stranger.

'Take 'em off now, Jilly,' whispered Paul, before he announced loudly, 'We'll let you know at the end of the show who the lucky new owner of the Christmas Kittens is to be—we'll have chosen them from your phone calls by then.'

There was more clapping. So our fate would be settled. What was going to become of us?

Chapter 10

Perdita Goes to the Deanery

All through the day I dozed in front of the gas fire. Although I was still exhausted, I felt very calm. In some way I knew this kind man, Tom the Verger, as he called himself, was going to help me. I no longer had the frenzied need to continue my quest for my brothers. And I was so very tired. But deep inside me I knew something good was going to happen when Tom returned.

Which he did, some time in the afternoon. He took off his strange black cloak and put on his overcoat instead.

'It's nippy out there, little Puss,' he said as he gently lifted me up. 'Snow's melting, thank goodness. Didn't stop people coming to the services, though. Really good turnouts, we had.'

As he talked he was wrapping me firmly in the blanket, so that I couldn't escape, even if I wanted to.

'Now, young lady, I'm taking you straight over to the Deanery. Dean'll be back from the Cathedral now. He'll sort out what's to be done with you.'

Without more ado he shut his front door behind us and walked across the snow-speckled grass. He called this place 'The Close', though I couldn't see anything close about it. It seemed to me a nice open space, very suitable for kitten games.

We reached the Deanery, which to me looked large and imposing, nearly as grand as the house where the posh cat lived. Tom went up the three white steps and with his free hand (the other was holding me) knocked on the knocker shaped like a curly fish. (I thought this was a good omen.) The door was opened almost immediately by a girl of school age with long brown plaits.

'Is your Pa home, Angela?'

Instead of answering his question, the girl held out her arms.

'Oh, Tom, you've brought a kitten. Where did you find him? Whose is he?'

By now she was hugging me, although I was still tightly wrapped in my blanket.

'Pardon me, Miss, but she's a her. I found her in the Cathedral last night. Set all the alarm bells off in her wandering. Must have spent the night in there.'

'Oh, Tom,' breathed Angela. 'She's a Christmas kitten.'

By now we'd moved into the hall. A door opened, and a tubby man joined the conversation. He had a ruddy complexion, and his head was bald except for a few straggling grey hairs on each side.

'What's this? What's all this? You found a kitten in the

93

Cathedral, Tom? Well, come in and sit down. Let's all be comfortable while we talk this over.'

The rosy-faced man, who was indeed the Dean, led the way into the room he'd just left. I was glad to see there was a roaring log fire.

Angela, still holding me, stood on the rug, and Tom and the Dean settled into cosy armchairs on either side of the hearth. Tom told the story of how he'd found me. I was beginning to feel sleepy all over again. I managed a few purrs, just to show that I found this place agreeable.

The Dean listened intently. He was wearing a black apron under his black coat, and black breeches that ended in leggings with buttons all up the sides. I thought I would quite like to play with all those buttons.

Angela interrupted Tom's explanation. 'Dad, we can keep her, can't we? You know you said we really needed a cat about the house.'

The Dean paused for a moment, thoughtfully fingering the large silver cross that was tucked into his cummerbund. 'We'll have to see, darling. It's true there's a mouse problem in these old houses. And I know you've been wanting a cat for a long time. But first we'll have to ring the police and see if anyone's missed her. I expect she's got an owner somewhere in the town.'

'Please, Dad—she's a stray. She wandered into the Cathedral looking for a place to sleep. She's lost. I know—we'll call her "Perdita", Shakespeare's "little lost one". We're doing *The Winter's Tale* at school this year.'

94

'That could be shortened to Perdy,' said the Dean doubtfully. And that was how I got my new name.

At that moment the door opened and a ginger-haired boy with freckles burst into the room. He was a year or two older than Angela.

'Dad, Dad, can we have the telly on? Please? It's Paul's Show. All the boys at school watch it. Please, Dad!'

'Oh, really Neil, I don't think now . . .'

But Angela, who'd put me down on the rug, making sure I was still comfortable, chimed in, 'Oh, please, Dad, let's watch. Paul usually has some animals looking for homes. I'm sure Tom would like to see it.'

'Tom, would you really care to watch with us?'

'It'd be a rare Christmas treat, Mr Dean, seeing as I don't have a telly.'

'Right you are then, we'll all watch.'

And the magic box, which I hadn't noticed standing in a corner, was moved forward and switched on. And there, behind the glass, was this thing they called 'Paul's Show'. To tell the truth, the Dean snoozed for a bit, and so did I. But we were rudely awoken by shouts from Angela and Neil, who were watching avidly. They'd both rushed over and were kneeling in front of the screen, jabbing at it with their fingers.

'It's our kitten!'

'It's Perdita!'

'Except there's two of them!'

'Look, Dad, they're exactly like her—just the same colouring.'

'Identical markings.'

'Look, Dad, white heart-shaped bib, white socklets, white hind stockings—they're identical to Perdy.'

Tom summed it all up.

'They must be her brothers,' he pronounced.

By now I'd joined the group round the magic box. Standing upright on my hind legs, I pressed my nose and forepaws against the glass just as I'd done outside that strange shop in the High Street. I had to believe my eyes—there were my beloved brothers, Peter and Pipkin. I could see them moving. But what was going to happen now?

I needn't have worried. Angela and Neil were shaking their father's arms.

'Please, Dad—ring up the TV station.'

'Now, this instant!'

'Say we'll have them and give them a good home!'

'Look, Perdita knows them. They're *her* brothers!'

'Dad, you must get them for her, they're *her* family!'

'Bless my soul—I really don't know—three cats . . .'

But the Dean was being hustled by his children towards the telephone in the hall. Neil was brandishing a piece of paper on which he'd written the number of the TV company.

While their father made the telephone call, Neil and Angela came back into the study. By now Tom was holding me on his knee, trying to soothe me. But I was so anxious, my hackles kept rising. Tom smoothed down the dark hair on my back.

'All shall be well, little Perdy,' he whispered. 'And all shall be well and all manner of thing shall be well.'

I felt comforted, although I didn't really know what was going on. Only that there was a chance, a slender chance, that I'd see my brothers again.

It seemed a long time before the Dean came back into the room. He was smiling broadly.

'We've got 'em. I was able to convince the TV people we've got their sister here, and that we could give them a good home. I think the address'—he chuckled to himself— 'may have helped. They'll be driven up from the TV place tomorrow.' He chucked me under the chin. 'You'll be reunited with your brothers!' The words I'd waited so long to hear.

The Dean continued 'What we'll do with *three* cats I really don't know. But now I must ring the police and find out if anyone's lost them.'

Chapter 11

The Christmas Feast

The Dean took quite a long time on the phone this time, too. And when he came back into the study he was smiling again.

'I've been talking to the most wonderful woman, Mrs Lovejoy. The police gave me her number—she lives on the outskirts of town. It seems Perdita and her brothers did belong to her, but she wanted good homes for them. She's just so relieved to know they're all safe and well, she's quite happy for us to have them, provided, of course, she comes to visit them from time to time. And that's easily arranged—I've asked her to dinner tomorrow night.'

'Our Christmas meal,' said the children together.

'What could be more fortunate? As you know, we always have our feast on Boxing Day—what with me being so busy with Christmas services in the Cathedral. So Mrs Lovejoy will be here to welcome her television kittens.'

'Great!' said Angela.

'Cool!' said Neil.

'Did she see them on the telly?' asked Angela, shaking her plaits and smoothing her blue cardigan.

'She's pretty chuffed,' the Dean was proud of himself for using this expression, 'at her kittens being famous.' He continued, 'And Tom, you'll come too, won't you? After all, it was you who found Perdita in the Cathedral.'

'We're having turkey and roast potatoes and all the trimmings,' said Neil.

'And Christmas pudding and brandy butter,' said his sister.

'Or ice cream for those that like it,' added Neil, knowing which he preferred.

'I'll look forward to it, thank you. Goodnight, then.' Tom gave me a final loving stroke. 'See you around,' he whispered.

I gathered I was going to see my beloved Mrs Lovejoy again, but after Tom had gone I began to feel rather lonely in this big new house. I needn't have worried though, becuse Angela seemed to sense how I was feeling about the strangeness of everything. First of all she gave me a delicate supper, and then, when it was her bedtime, she took me upstairs with her. While I could hear her splashing about in the bathroom I had a good sniff round her room—all the smells were interesting. And when Angela jumped into bed, I leapt up onto the duvet beside her.

'Oh Perdy, I do miss Mum so much,' she told me as she stroked me. 'It's just a year since she died. But now you've come to keep me company. And tomorrow your brothers will be here too.'

Then we both fell asleep. I dreamt that I was still searching for Peter and Pipkin, and my whole body twitched as I slept.

But when I woke I realised the dream I'd lived for so long was over. Angela jumped out of bed, saying, 'Perdy, come on! Your brothers are arriving today. They're being driven all the way up from the TV station. They thought we were the best possible home for them—mostly because we're so sure you're all related. Their markings are just the same as yours, Perdy. You must have been triplets!'

She said all this as she dressed quickly, throwing on her jeans and T-shirt.

'Hurry, hurry, darling Perdy, we've so much to do getting everything ready.'

She scampered down the wide staircase, and I lolloped behind her. After breakfast everyone seemed busy, so I had a chance to explore my new home. I investigated every nook and cranny. It was a big, old-fashioned house but, I decided, quite a suitable home for three cats. From the windows I saw that there was a large rather overgrown garden with many shrubs. What lovely games we would have out there when the weather improved, I thought. I lingered for a long time on the staircase—it was ideal for kitten play.

Neil, who didn't seem as busy as everyone else, stopped to talk to me. He produced some lumps of sugar from his pocket and threw them up and down the stairs. Gleefully, I chased after them.

'Perdy,' he said, when I finally lay panting with exhaustion on the bottom step, 'once the shops open again I'll get you some ping-pong balls for proper games. It'll be great!'

Then, at last, the longed-for moment arrived. A very grand black car drew up outside the Deanery, and a man in a smart uniform with a peaked cap knocked loudly on the fish knocker. (I was watching this from the study window.)

Angela opened the door, but the driver handed the travelling box, with a slight bow, to the Dean.

'The Television Kittens, m'lud,' said the man, and the Dean raised his eyebrows in surprise at the sudden elevation of his status. 'With the compliments of the TV company, who hopes as they'll have a very good home wiv you and your family. If you wouldn't mind just signing here, sir . . .'

The Dean scribbled at the bottom of the piece of paper the man was holding out.

'Thank you, sir. That puts everything in order. Wishing you all a good day.' And with another bow, he returned to the grand car and drove away.

Very carefully, the Dean carried the box into the study and put it down on the hearth rug, where I was waiting. My yellow eyes were very wide and my black tail very erect, and my whiskers were all a-twitch. How I'd waited and longed for this moment!

Neil lifted Peter out, and Angela reached for Pipkin. For a moment we stared at each other, and then there were mutual mews of recognition. My brothers had grown and were definitely fatter. Realising I would be Mother now, I gave them a quick lick and they purred in appreciation.

Then we all curled up and settled down on the rug.

'There you are!' said Angela. 'Of course they're Perdy's brothers. Look at them greeting each other.'

'If they'd been strangers I suppose they would have fought,' said her brother. (How stupid human beings are sometimes.)

'Alike as three peas,' observed the Dean, gazing fondly down at us.

We lay together in front of the fire, and my brothers began to tell me about their adventures. They weren't the least little bit interested in mine.

Then our beloved Mrs Lovejoy arrived. She swept us up in her arms and smothered us with kisses. This embarrassed us a bit, but as we'd all thought we would never see her again, we were really delighted.

Tom came soon after, and was enthusiastically introduced to Peter and Pipkin. But somehow, deep down, I knew that I would always be his special favourite. So he cradled me while Mrs Lovejoy talked to my brothers.

'*My* kittens! Well, Fozzy's really. She sends her regards, by the way. But who'd have thought you'd have become so famous—there you were on the TV! I couldn't believe my eyes when I first saw you! I kept saying, "Is it my Peter and Pipkin?" Stars you are now—d'you realise that?'

Rather sickeningly, both my brothers rolled over, showing their white tummies, while Mrs L. (who was kneeling beside them) stroked their soft fur. Privately I decided that later on, when things had settled, I would take them down a peg or two. Already they were using all sorts of strange phrases they'd obviously picked up in that weird place they'd been taken to. They kept saying they'd won the 'Euro-Pussy Prize', which was just something silly they'd invented. And they talked about 'going into make-up' when they wanted to be brushed. Tomorrow I'd put a stop to all that nonsense and bring them back to cat-level again.

The Dean was explaining to Mrs Lovejoy how Tom had found me in the Cathedral, and they thought I'd been there all night.

'Why, I came up to the carol service,' said Mrs L. 'It was lovely. Fancy my little Polly, I mean Perdy, being there all the time. To think I might have seen her!'

'And taken her home,' said Neil, who'd been listening. 'Jolly good thing you didn't. Otherwise none of this would have happened.'

Just then Angela announced that supper was ready, and we all trooped into the dining room. And what a sight met our eyes: holly and paper chains everywhere, and in the corner of the room a huge fir tree, hung with wonderful sparkling balls. It was too much for us—with our kitten's instincts we three dashed between people's legs and hurled ourselves at the tree, batting and pouncing on those delicious tinkling decorations. There was a crash and the sound of smashing glass as the tree fell over on top of us.

'Whoops!' cried Neil.

'Are you all right?' asked Angela, picking me out of the fallen debris and dusting me down.

'I'm so sorry!' said Mrs Lovejoy. 'Your beautiful tree ruined.

I do apologise for them. That was very naughty,' she lectured, as she rescued Peter and Pipkin.

Tom didn't say anything at all, but he righted the tree and scooped all the shards of broken glass into the big flowerpot in which the tree was planted.

Then the meal was served. Angela brought the enormous turkey in from the kitchen and the Dean carved. Neil handed round the vegetables. An extra chair had been pulled up to the table so that we three kittens could sit and watch all that was going on. Our nostrils whiffled in anticipation, and I stared at the flickering candle flame in front of me and thought of all the adventures we'd had.

Mrs Lovejoy whispered to me, 'I'll visit you. The Dean says I can come over as often as I like. You've got a lovely home here, Perdy.' She was gradually getting used to my new name.

Then it was our turn to feast.

Neil laid three saucers at the front of the now-ruined tree. There was one thing we were all agreed on: the turkey was very, very good.